Loaves and Fish

THE REST OF THE STORY

Written by: Valerie A. Nichols

Illustrated by: Curtis Newman

To order additional copies of this book, contact:
Xlibris
844-714-8691
www.Xlibris.com
Orders@Xlibris.com

ISBN: Softcover   978-1-6641-6676-9
        Hardcover   978-1-6641-6677-6
        EBook   978-1-6641-6678-3

Library of Congress Control Number: 2021906667

Print information available on the last page

Rev. date: 04/06/2021

Note to Readers from the Author

Like a mother or father trying to decide on names for their child, it was very important to me that I choose names that I felt "fit" my characters. So, I give you the names and their meanings below. As you read the story, see if you agree with what I chose!

You probably already know that the **TITLE** of a book or story is as important as the characters! **Before** you read, and **as** you read, ask yourself what the words, "The Rest of the Story" could mean.

You will come across the word "Hoopoe" in the story! Funny sounding, isn't it? Have someone help you find the meaning of that word AND the sound it makes, which I think is beautiful!! You artists might even try to draw it!! **V. Nichols**

Characters' Names and their Meanings

Amnon—Faithful

Hannah—Favor or Grace

Nathan—Gift of God or He will give

Asher—Blessed or Happy

Okay, it's time to read the story! ENJOY!

Loaves and Fish: The Rest of the Story

Nathan could hardly wait for today's family adventure to start! Jesus would be on the mountain today. Nathan was curious to see the man people said came from God. Best of all, Nathan's friend Asher and his family were going, too! It would take a few hours to reach Bethsaida and having his friend along would make the trip go faster. Outside, Nathan's father, Amnon, was closing two goat skins with water for the trip. Nathan ran out to him.

"Father! May I bring my sling shot so Asher and I can practice our aim along the way?"

"No, you may not, Nathan." Amnon faced his son. "Many people will be travelling with us on the road today. It's best you leave it at home."

"All right, Father." Nathan turned to go inside, when he heard, "NATHAN!!" His friend was waving wildly a short distance away.

"Father! Look! Here comes Asher's family!" He ran into the house.

"Mother! They're coming! Hurry!" Hannah smiled, barely able to finish wrapping up some fish and barley bread before Nathan grabbed the bundle and ran to join his friend whose family was just passing their home.

The journey had begun!

As the morning went on, families from other villages joined the procession. Clouds of dust floated around the crowd's feet as they walked along the desert roads.

Some adults sang, children laughed, and Nathan and Asher chattered back and forth like cactus wrens. Both boys loved the desert birds and often practiced their calls. Sometimes, one boy would yell, "Challenge! Crested Lark!" Then the other boy had to "sing" like the bird. If he couldn't, he lost the challenge.

After a few hours, Nathan sensed a difference in the crowd. People walked a little faster. Voices were talking louder. Nathan nudged his friend's arm. "Look!" Ahead, a mountain was rising out of the flatness of the desert.

"Oh, good. We're almost there, Nathan! Let's finish the Challenge with one last call each. Me first! House Sparrow!"

"Cheep, cheep, cheep-cheep-cheep!" Nathan sang in a high voice. "MY turn. Hoopoe!"

Asher frowned. " Hoopoe? I don't remember THAT call! You win again!"

Reaching the base of the mountain, families joyfully greeted their friends from other towns. Children ran to play with other children. Men worked their way forward to sit in the front; women and children sat behind.

Nathan looked around. "Something's different."

Asher laughed. "Oh, did you see a Hoopoe?!"

"No, listen. Do you hear that?" Both boys turned toward the people.

Several men were pointing toward a man; Nathan heard the name, "Jesus," whispered throughout the crowd. Jesus moved among the people, talking to some as he passed. Nathan's eyes became fixed on the man's steady, calm steps as he walked up the hill.

Men motioned for quiet. "Shhhh, Shhh. Teacher's going to talk!"

The women gathered the children and began to settle them down.

Nathan and Asher went back to their mothers.

Sh-hh!

Teacher raised his hands. Then He spoke.

"I am the light of the world. He who follows me shall not walk in darkness, but shall have the light of life."

The men were quiet, listening closely to everything Teacher said.

"For whoever does the will of my Father which is in heaven... is my brother and sister and mother...."

Nathan *tried* to listen, but after a while, he only wanted to get up—move—talk with Asher.

"Give and it shall be given to you pressed down, running over...."

Nathan turned to his mother.

"Mother, could Asher and I walk to the back of all the women's and children's groups and then walk back?"

"No, Nathan," Hannah replied. "You and Asher will have enough walking when we return home." Nathan sat down, put his fists deep into his cheeks and stared at his sandals.

Early afternoon turned into late afternoon. Nathan had been standing or sitting near this hill all day, and now he was tired...and hungry.

"Mama," he pulled on his mother's dress. "Are we leaving soon? I want to play more with Asher before it gets dark."

"Hush," Hannah spoke quietly. "We will leave when Teacher is finished speaking."

Nathan held up his small cloth bundle. "Well," he whispered back, eyes pleading, "may I eat the food I brought?"

His mother's eyes burned like the coals of a fire. "When Teacher is finished speaking!"

Nathan knew better than to say anything more, so he tucked his lunch under his arm and sat back down on a scraggily patch of brush.

Then, just as suddenly as silence had fallen on the crowd earlier, Nathan now heard murmuring. He looked up. No one was leaving, but the men who had sat closest to Teacher were walking through the crowd calling out something. When they got closer to their section, Nathan heard a man yell, **"Does anyone have any food?"**

Nathan jumped up. "**I do!**" he shouted, holding up his small lunch.

The man came over quickly. Smiling, he said, "Hello. My name is Andrew. What do you have?"

"Five loaves and two fish!" Nathan said proudly.

"May I have it?" Andrew bent down. "What's **your** name?"

Nathan held his bundle tighter. "Nathan." His stomach was rumbling a little.

"Well, Nathan," Andrew began, "it would be a great gift to God if you would let Teacher bless it."

Nathan thought a moment. "Teacher would want this?"

"Oh, very much!" Andrew assured him.

"Well...." Nathan thought about his stomach, then Teacher, then Andrew's words-- 'A great gift to God'. He held the cloth bag up with both hands. "Here, take it!"

"Thank you Nathan!" Andrew took the lunch and raced through the crowd toward Jesus.

Nathan shook his head in wonder as he watched Andrew run up the hill. What could one lunch do?

What happened next left Nathan speechless.

Nathan saw Andrew give the bundle to a man called Peter, who gave it to Teacher!

Teacher held it up. He thanked God and blessed Nathan's offering; then, he broke off pieces of the small loaves and gave some to each of his friends.

Nathan frowned. "Well, that won't go far, and I sure won't get any of my lunch back," he grumbled as he patted his stomach.

Suddenly, he heard shouts from the crowd.

"Thank you, Jesus! Praise God! Thank you, thank you!"

Nathan looked up. His mouth opened, but no sound came out! Some of Jesus's friends held full baskets of bread! They were passing the baskets to the men first and then to the women and children. But, even as people took bread, more bread seemed to refill the basket. After several minutes, when the basket reached Nathan, he grabbed a handful of bread while quickly looking in—and under—the basket. How could this be?

Then, after everyone had bread, the same thing happened with the fish! Grown men were laughing in delight at having full bellies. Everyone began laughing. Some people danced. Birds swooped down for crumbs.

Finally, Teacher told the crowd they should go home before it got dark. Families and neighbors regrouped and---still talking and laughing---headed back down the hill. Nathan watched eagerly for his father. He wondered if his father knew it was **his** lunch Teacher had blessed!

At that moment, he felt a hand on his shoulder. "Father!" Nathan called out and turned. But it was **not** his father who stood in front of him. It was **Teacher**!

Looking directly into Nathan's eyes, squeezing his shoulder lightly, Jesus smiled. "Thank you, Nathan, for sharing your food. Your gift gave God the materials to be a great blessing today."

Nathan looked down. He wasn't sure what to say. Should he thank Teacher or just say, "You're welcome"? Nathan felt a light tap on his shoulder. "Teacher, I...." He looked back up.

"No, Nathan," Amnon laughed. "Just your father."

Nathan grabbed his father's arm. "Did you see Teacher?"

"Why, yes, he's heading back up the hill. He nodded to me. I think he's tired from his teaching. It's been a long day, and we need to start back ourselves."

"But Father! Did you know the loaves and fish were mine?"

"Now, Nathan," Amnon began and looked at his wife. Hannah glanced back at her husband, silently nodding "yes" to him.

The crowd was moving past them, praising or singing to God. When Asher's family passed, Asher yelled, "I'll see you tomorrow!" But Nathan didn't answer.

Amnon looked at his son, studying his face. He put his arm around Nathan's shoulders. "Well, you've had quite a day. You must tell me all about it as we walk home. I must admit," he added, grinning at Hannah, "I didn't realize what a fine lunch your mother can prepare!"

One week later, Nathan remembered the words Jesus had said: "Your gift gave God the materials to be a great blessing today."

"Mother, Asher told me his mother's not feeling well. May I take them our extra oil with some of the cakes you made for us today?"

"Of course! What a thoughtful thing to do, Nathan." Hannah walked over to give her son a hug. "I'll put some cakes and the oil in a basket right away."

Years later, Nathan and Asher replaced a damaged wagon wheel for a man who had broken his leg. "Thank you so much, boys! My harvest overflowed this year, and now my son and I can take our grain to the market. Please, each of you take two baskets for your family."

Nathan continued to provide "materials" whenever and wherever he felt they could help. How much they might help, he'd leave up to God. But he knew one thing for sure.

God's blessings would always provide more than enough!

Did you know the story continues today? What can YOU share with someone today so God can bless them?

Time to listen?   **Food**?   **Talent**?

DRAW something you could do for someone TODAY!
(friend, neighbor, parent, teacher, coach)

Printed in the United States
by Baker & Taylor Publisher Services